We're Going on a
LEAF HUNT

by Steve Metzger

Illustrated by Miki Sakamoto

3520004524

SCHOLASTIC INC.

New York   Toronto   London   Auckland   Sydney
Mexico City   New Delhi   Hong Kong   Buenos Aires

To My Best Girls—

Julia, Nancy, and Lopey

—S.M.

ISBN-13: 978-0-439-87377-2
ISBN-10: 0-439-87377-0

Text copyright © 2005 by Steve Metzger.
Illustrations copyright © 2005 by Miki Sakamoto.

10 9 8 7 6 5 4 3 2 1   8 9 10 11 12/0
Printed in the U.S.A.
This edition first printing, August 2008

We're going on a leaf hunt. We're going right away.

Let's find **colorful** leaves.

It's a wonderful day!

We're coming to a mountain—
a TALL, TALL mountain.

We can't go under it. We have to go over it!

We're coming to a mountain.

Come on, let's go!

Climb, climb,

huff, puff,

We made it!

Pick up those leaves from the **maple** tree!

We're going on a leaf hunt.

We're going right away.

Let's find **colorful** leaves.

It's a wonderful day!

We're coming to a forest—
a dark, dark forest.

We can't go over it.

We have to go through it!

We're coming to a forest.

Come on, let's go!

Step, step, squish, squash.
We made it!

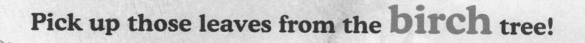

Pick up those leaves from the birch tree!

We're going on a leaf hunt.

We're going right away.

Let's find **colorful** leaves.

It's a wonderful day!

We're coming to a waterfall—
a swooshing, swooshing waterfall.

We can't go through it.
We have to go around it!
We're coming to a waterfall.
Come on, let's go!

Slip, slide, splish, splash.
We made it!

Pick up those leaves from the hickory tree!

We're going on a leaf hunt.
We're going right away.

Let's find **colorful** leaves.

It's a wonderful day!

We're coming to a lake—
a **cold**, cold lake.

We can't go around it.
We have to go across it!
We're coming to a lake.
Come on, let's go!

Row, row,

plip,

plop!

We made it!

Pick up those leaves from the **red oak** tree!

What's that sound?
It's coming from that bush!

It's **black.** It's white.
It's **black** *and* white.

It's a...a...**skunk**!

LET'S GO!

Back across the lake…

plip, plop.

Back past the waterfall...

splish, splash.

Back through the forest . . .

squish, squash.

Back over the mountain...

huff, puff.

We're home!

We went on a leaf hunt.

What a wonderful day!

We found lots of **colorful** leaves.

Now let's **jump** and **play**!